Picture Fables Collection
Paul White

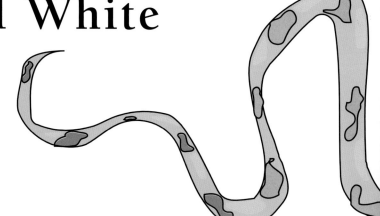

Illustrated by Peter Oram

Jungle Doctor Picture Fables Collection

Donkey Wisdom 4

Famous Monkey Last Words 26

Monkey in a Lion's Skin 48

Reflections of Hippo 70

The Cool Pool 92

The Monkeys and the Eggs 114

Monkey Crosses the Equator 136

Sweet and Sour Hippo 158

Copyright © Estate of Paul White 1997
Illustrated by Peter Oram

Jungle Doctor Picture Fables Collection first published in the UK 1997 by OM Publishing

03 02 01 00 99 98 97   7 6 5 4 3 2 1

OM Publishing is an imprint of Paternoster Publishing,
P.O. Box 300, Carlisle, Cumbria, CA3 0QS, U.K.

British Library Cataloguing in Publication Data

A catalogue record for this book is available from the British Library

ISBN 1-85078-267-9

Printed in Singapore by SNP Printing Pte Ltd.

Donkey Wisdom

Punda, the donkey, was unhappy.

"It isn't fair," he said. "Simba, the lion, has beautiful tawny skin. Twiga, the giraffe, is golden and mottled like the sunlight and shadow under thorn-trees. But *I'm just black.*"

"What's wrong with that?" said monkey. "It doesn't show the dirt, does it, hippo?"

Boohoo shook his head. "And — um — it's useful. On dark nights lions and leopards can't see you."

Donkey sighed. "How I wish I could change my colour!"

"There's one place in the jungle where wishes come true," smiled Toto.

Boohoo mumbled, "I don't — um — think you should tell him. It's spooky and if he goes there — um . . ."

"His wish might come true," chuckled Toto.

"Where is it?" demanded Punda. "Tell me. Where do wishes come true?"

"It's a magic cave," said Toto.

"Then come on. Let's go."

"Um, do you think it's wise?" asked Boohoo.

"Of course it isn't," said Toto, shivering. "But it could be an adventure."

"Then please take me," begged Punda. "If wishes come true I wish I was white. Wouldn't it be wonderful to be a dazzling, white donkey?"

"Oh dear," panted Boohoo. "It's a long way. My poor feet are . . ."

"Stop grumbling," shouted Toto. "There's the cave. In you go, Punda, and start wishing."

Donkey's voice trembled. "It looks dark in there."

"Yes," said Boohoo. "Dark and clammy – um – there's still time to change your mind."

"Oh, shush," chuckled Toto. "Keep quiet, Boohoo. Punda is big enough to take care of himself. Donkey, do you or don't you want to be white?"

"Yes, I do," said Punda. "I do. I do."

"Then come to the cave and make a wish."

"Let's all go together," said Punda, his teeth chattering.
"Um — but I haven't any wishes to make, none at all," chuckled
Boohoo. "And Toto, if you went into that cave and heard
creepy noises, you'd — um — turn white before he would."
Toto sniffed. "You're very brave, outside the cave. Eh, that's
poetry."
"Stop making all that noise," breathed donkey.
"I'm going in."
After they had waited a long minute Boohoo said, "You shouldn't
have told him about this cave. You have a big mouth."
Toto's eyes stuck out. "Look who's talking, You could eat
a whole watermelon sideways."

12

"Look at me," came donkey's voice loudly

"Um – eh – ooh?" gulped Hippo.

Monkey jumped up and down. "He's white. Donkey's really *white* white! Hey! How did you change colour, Punda?"

"I went into the dark cave and I called out, 'I wish I was white.' And now I am

I'm the only white donkey in the jungle. Do you like my new colour, Toto?"

"It'll show the dirt. You'll never keep it clean."

"I'll be very careful," said Punda, hopefully.

"Mm," mused Toto. "But you won't stay white for long. You'll be a sort of dirty grey. That's the best of being black. It doesn't show the dirt."

"Oh dear," sighed Punda. "For a while the others will admire me, but when I look grey and grubby they'll laugh. I wish I was black again."

15

"Where's he going?" asked Boohoo.

"Back to the cave to wish again. He seems to want to be black," said Toto.

"He does have – um – trouble making up his mind, doesn't he?" replied hippo. "And it's all your fault, you muddle-headed monkey. You brought us all the way for nothing. You ought to be - eh - what's that?"

"Toto, Boohoo," shouted donkey. "Look, I'm back again and black again."

"Um," nodded Boohoo. "That's the donkey we know. What a – um – beautiful, black beast."

Donkey tossed his head. "I'm glad you like it. Black's a good colour, don't you think, Toto?"

"Yes, but it's very common."

"What do you mean?" demanded donkey.

"Well," said Toto, scratching his head, "every donkey you see is black. If you want to stand out you have to be different."

Donkey stamped his feet. "But you said . . ."

"I know. I know," nodded Toto. "That was before I had time to think about it. You were quite right. Black is dull and not very attractive."

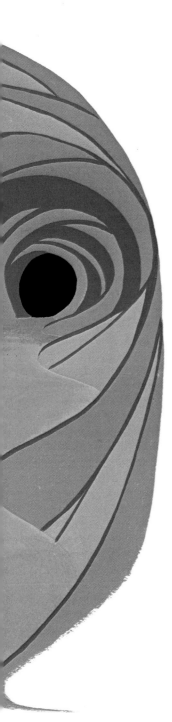

Donkey was most upset. "Then I'll go back and wish again."

Toto shouted, "I'll come with you."

"Can I come too?" asked Boohoo.

Toto laughed. "I don't think you'll ever come to."

"Ohh." Boohoo's voice sounded boomy and queer. "It's dark."

"Hullo," shouted Toto. The echo came back, H-U-L-L-O!

"Don't d-d-do that," said Boohoo. "You'll wake up the spooks!"

"Punda, start wishing quickly – ooH! – what's that?" said Toto.

"You walked right into me," said donkey.

"Well, it's so dark and you're so black."

"As I said before," mumbled Boohoo, "black is a good colour when you don't want lions to see you at night."

"But I want to be white," shouted Punda.

"That's very dangerous," said hippo, shaking his head.

"Oh," gulped donkey. "Then I wish I was black."

"Then you'd just be like any other donkey," sniffed Toto.

"Oh, dear," yelled donkey. "Then I wish I was white . . .

or black . . .

no, white,

that is, black."

The echo came back, Black! White! Black! White!

21

Suddenly there was
a vast rumbling. "What's happening?
gulped hippo. "Quickly," shouted Tot
"The roof's falling in.
Let's get out.
O-U-T!"

Hippo sneezed. "Hipp, Hipp, Hip — oschoo!"

"Please," said Toto. "Please mind where you're blowing."

"Sorry," snorted Boohoo. "Dust always makes me sneeze and wheeze!"

"What about my fur?" retorted Toto. "Dirt all over me."

"Ha ha ha ha," laughed Toto.

"Ho ho ho ho," chuckled Boohoo.

"What's so funny?" demanded donkey.

"Ha ha, you're black and white

and you're white and black, ho ho,

and black and white, ha ha!"

"Oh NO!" groaned Punda.

"I'm stripes all over me. I must wish again."

"It's too late. The cave fell in just as
we got out," grinned Toto.

Punda shook his head. "Oh, why can't
I make up my mind!"

Now you know what a zebra is — a donkey
who can't make up his mind.

The most important thing anyone can do is
to decide to ask Jesus to forgive their
sin, and to give them everlasting life.

Read about it in:

The Gospel of John chapter 3, verse 16
and Romans chapter 10, verses 9, 10 and 11.

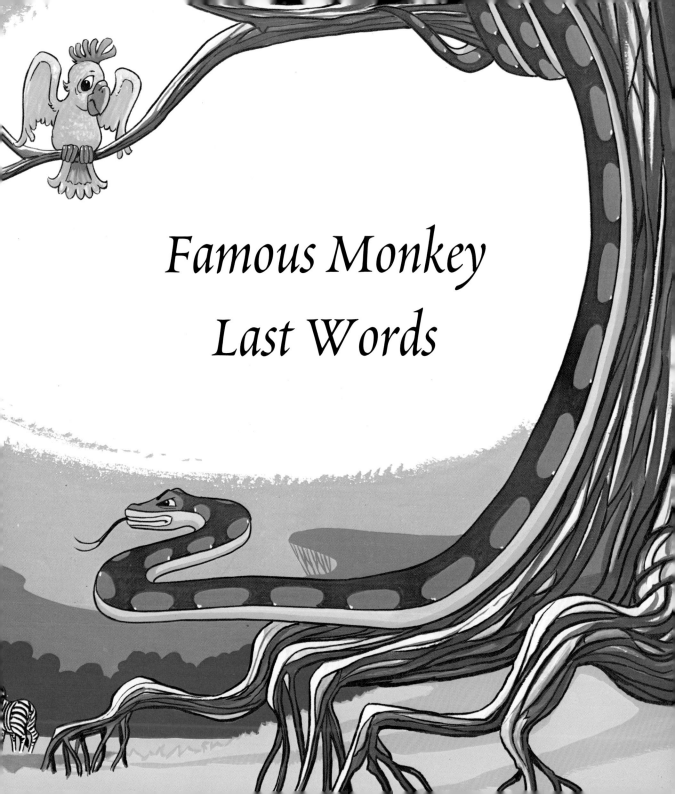

Famous Monkey
Last Words

Toto, the monkey, was sitting up in a tree trying very hard to listen to his teacher, Twiga, the giraffe.

But it wasn't easy. His toes were itchy and he wanted to play with butterflies.

Twiga said firmly, "You must listen, Toto. It's very important to learn three special rules.

One day they could save your life."

Toto yawned, but Twiga said earnestly, "Life is often dangerous and you MUST KNOW these rules.
Obey the laws of the jungle and you'll be safe.
Disobey them and you'll be in trouble."

"I know the first already," boasted Toto. "IF YOU SMELL A LEOPARD, CLIMB A TREE AND GO OUT ON A THIN LIMB."

Twiga nodded. "Good; and the second one says, DON'T STAND AT THE BACK OF A ZEBRA."

"But," said Toto, "I haven't even seen a zebra."

"You will soon," said Twiga. "Remember specially: NEVER stand at the back of a zebra."

"Why?" asked Toto.

"If a zebra kicks you it will hurt and HURT," said Twiga.

"Wow! I wouldn't like that," laughed little monkey.
"And, Twiga, what's the third rule?"

"DON'T LOOK INTO A SNAKE'S EYES. Now can you tell me the three jungle rules, Toto?"

"If I tell you them all can I go and play?"

Twiga nodded.

"I can do it," said Toto.

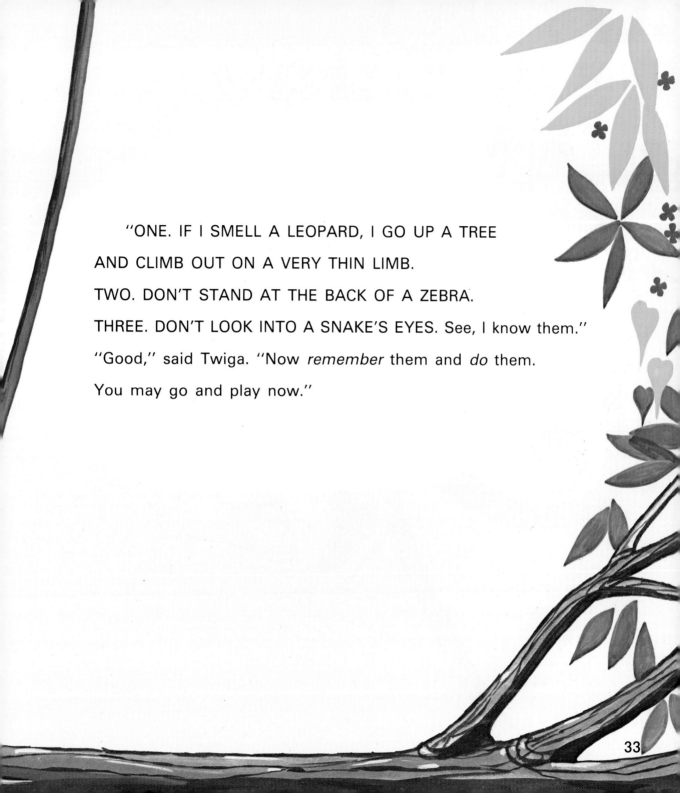

"ONE. IF I SMELL A LEOPARD, I GO UP A TREE
AND CLIMB OUT ON A VERY THIN LIMB.
TWO. DON'T STAND AT THE BACK OF A ZEBRA.
THREE. DON'T LOOK INTO A SNAKE'S EYES. See, I know them."

"Good," said Twiga. "Now *remember* them and *do* them.
You may go and play now."

Toto was having fun swinging on jungle vines.

He heard a deep voice, "Um, good morning, monkey."

"Hullo, Boohoo. Have you ever seen a zebra?"

Hippo nodded his large head. "Um, yes. A black horse with white stripes, or is it a white horse with black stripes? It's hard to remember."

Toto laughed. "Do you know where one is?"

"Er, yes. If you're very quiet I will show you. Eh, oh, splendid. Look over there."

Monkey was delighted. "So that's a zebra. Does he bite?"

"Er, no, Toto. He's a very quiet animal really.

It isn't his teeth you have to keep away from.

It's his back feet."

"Does he run very fast, Boohoo?"

"I don't know," said hippo, slowly.

"Can he go as fast as giraffe?"

"I don't know," said hippo.

Monkey was excited. "Let's make him run and find out."

"Watch him go, Boohoo."

Hippo gasped. "Put down those thorns!
Um, Toto, stop it at once. Er, um,
I can't bear to look . . ."

"WATCH THIS, BOOHOO!"

Two flying hooves hit him. WHACK!

He sailed through the air . . . . .

38

. . . . and landed THUD!!

Boohoo went over to Toto. "Oh, um, are you all right?"
There was no answer.

"Um, Toto, speak to me." Monkey opened his eyes and
groaned. "Um, you were kicked by a zebra. Er, I will call
Twiga. He will know what to do. Um, I'll hurry."

Toto sat sadly holding his head.

There was a swishing noise behind him.

A soft voice said, "Is s-s-s-something the matter?"

"Yes," mumbled Toto. "A silly zebra kicked me."

"I'm s-s-sorry to hear that," said the voice.

"I can't see you," groaned Toto. "My eyes are funny and my head aches and aches."

"I'll come closer then. Now, can you s-s-s-see me?"

Toto blinked. "Stop swaying about like that. Who are you?"

"I'm s-s-snake. You really are s-s-sick.

Let me hold you tight.

Look into my eyes.

Gaze into them.

You feel s-s-so s-s-sleepy."

Little monkey yawned. "So s-shut your eyes and s-s-sleep now."

Twiga and Boohoo came running up.

Giraffe said, "Snake has put Toto to sleep."

"Snake, don't you hurt that monkey," Boohoo called loudly.

Snake hissed. "Go away or I'll bite you."

"You'll bite me, eh?" chuckled Boohoo.

"You aren't the only one who can bite.

Would you like me to show you?"

Snake wriggled off as fast as he could go.

45

Twiga spoke gently to monkey. "Wake up."

"What's happening?" said Toto.

"You've been doing what I told you not to do.
You looked into his eyes.
Snake nearly had you for his dinner."

"He seemed so friendly," said Toto.

"Was he?" said Twiga. "Tell me, what is the
third rule of the jungle?"

"I remember *now*," said Toto, softly. "I didn't
do what I was told. Sorry."

Jesus means God saves. This tells us who
he is (God) and what he does (saves). The
way to eternal life is to trust him and
to obey him. People who love God obey him.
Jesus himself said "If you love me, do what
I tell you." John chapter 14, verse 15.

"It's only monkey wisdom to run round in a moth-eaten lion's skin and say you're a lion."

Everyone, except Boohoo the hippo, thought it was a lovely day in the jungle. Boohoo had a question that went round and round in his head.

"Um, Twiga," he said to giraffe, "do lions climb trees?"

"They do sometimes," said Twiga.

"Ooh, good," nodded hippo. "Look at that one. He was swinging by his – um – tail a minute ago. Um, do you think he's ferocious?"

"I think we're safe," smiled Twiga. "Let's say good morning."

"Hallo up there," called hippo.

51

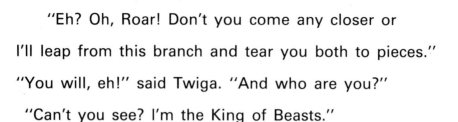

"Eh? Oh, Roar! Don't you come any closer or

I'll leap from this branch and tear you both to pieces."

"You will, eh!" said Twiga. "And who are you?"

"Can't you see? I'm the King of Beasts."

"Toto, it's only monkey wisdom to run round in a moth-eaten

lion's skin and say you're a lion."

"Don't talk to me like that, giraffe, or I'll eat you.

I'm not a monkey any more. I've become a lion. I do what lions do.

I eat what lions eat. I say what lions say – Roar! And

I go where lions go."

Twiga spoke gently.

"You can't become a lion by imitating lions."

"Oh?" mumbled Boohoo.

"Oh no?" shouted Toto. "This lion skin fits perfectly.
I'm noble and fierce and . . ."

"To become a lion," went on Twiga, "you would have to be
born all over again and become a new creature."

55

But Toto was taking no notice. He strode along snarling. "Watch my lion-like steps, Boohoo," he roared. "Aren't I clever? I wonder how many smart animals there are in the jungle."

"There's one less than you think," said Twiga. "You could be playing a very dangerous game."

Hippo nodded slowly. "If you – um – meet other animals, what will happen then?"

Toto chortled, "I met hyaena this morning. He took one look at me and bolted. He knows a lion when he sees one."

"But what happens," asked Twiga, "if you meet a bad-tempered rhino or a hungry leopard?"

Toto made growling noises. "What will they see?
Me, the King of the Jungle. When they hear me growl
they'll tremble. When they hear me roar, they'll run."

"Um," thought Boohoo, "perhaps the best way to

teach a monkey something is to let him find out for himself."

His nose suddenly sent him a warning.

"Oops, look out, everyone. Leopard is coming.

Quick, Toto, up into a tree before he sees you.

Come on, Twiga."

"Do what Boohoo says," called Twiga. "You can play lions later."

But Toto sniffed. "I'm not frightened even if you are.

Leopard knows what to expect from lions. ROAR!

Bye-bye, Boohoo. Hide if you're scared."

"So leopard's coming, is he?

I'll let him know who's here. ROAR — ROAR."

He shook his mane and grinned.

"That should send a shiver up his spine."

Leopard growled.

"Who did that?" demanded Toto.

Leopard growled again.

"Run, monkey!" shouted Twiga.

"Run fast!" bellowed Boohoo.

Toto turned and looked at leopard.

The leopard growled deep in his throat.

Toto's voice suddenly became squeaky. "Stay where you are.

Nice pussy. Stand back. Stand back, I say. Am I

the King of Beasts or . . . HELP!"

The lion's skin fell off

Toto rushed up a tree and far out on a limb.

Leopard sat waiting and watching.

He waited all day, thinking all the time of monkey for dinner.

Leopard was still waiting when the sun set and the moon rose,

and then, while he had a very small snooze,

Twiga ran underneath the tree

and Toto escaped by the skin of his teeth.

As giraffe galloped away, Toto said,

"You saved me; thank you, Twiga."

Then in a small voice, "I was wrong, and you don't become a

lion by doing things or saying things or wearing things."

"That was only monkey wisdom," agreed Twiga.

Real wisdom is understanding that when anyone becomes

a Christian he becomes a new person altogether. He has

been born again, a new life has begun. He has become

one of God's family. See what it means to become new?

Read 2 Corinthians chapter 5, verse 17.

Reflections of Hippo

Toto smiled. "Dic-Dic, antelope, I've found a delicious coconut. Boohoo, the hippo, will crack it open for us . . . I hope. He has the biggest jaws in the jungle."

They found their friend in a shallow part of the river.

"Boohoo," yelled monkey. "It's good to see you."

"I don't think he heard," said Dic-Dic.

Toto looked carefully. "Maybe he's asleep. No, his eyes are open. I'll go and see what's up."

Toto's voice was full of cheerfulness. "Boohoo, my dear fat friend . . ."

"Oh, you've spoiled it all," grumbled Boohoo. "I've been standing here waiting for the water to become very still. He told me, 'When the water is very still you can see your face in it.' "

"Who told you?" asked Toto.

73

"A dear old monkey. He said, 'Boohoo, when the water is very still, look into it and you'll see your face.' "

Toto laughed. "And scare the life out of yourself."

Dic-Dic spoke gently. "Boohoo, we're sorry we disturbed the water, but why did you want to see your face?"

"Oh," smiled hippo. "That dear old monkey said I was handsome and I want to see how good-looking I am."

"Where did you find that old monkey?" grinned Toto. "Sitting in the hot sun?"

"Eh, no, that is he was standing on the river bank. He couldn't get across. It's deep, you see, and he couldn't swim. He said, 'What a handsome hippopotamus.'"

Toto nodded slowly, then he said, "He could see you were not only handsome but a good swimmer and kind and thoughtful as well."

"Ye-es," smiled Boohoo. "Fancy him knowing all those things about me without even seeing me before."

Toto's eyes twinkled. "So he said all those nice things about you and you helped him with a ride across the river. Now I want you to help me.

"See this coconut? Please crack it open for me."

"He was such a nice monkey," mumbled Boohoo. " 'A handsom[e] hippo,' he said. He was my friend."

"I'm your friend, too," said Toto. "Haven't I ever told you how handsome you are?"

"Not ever and that means NEVER," said Boohoo, loudly.

"Oh, I thought you knew and I didn't want you to be conceited. Boo, when I look into your face I see character. I see courage. I see strength."

"How can you see all those things in my face?" asked hippo.

"I read between the lines," laughed Toto.

"Please crack open our coconut," said Dic-Dic.

"*No I won't,*" grumbled Boohoo. "I'm going to find some still water and look at myself."

"If you want to look at your face," said Toto, "I'll bring you a mirror. If I let you look into it and see yourself will you crack open our coconut?"

"After I've seen myself," said Boohoo.

Toto brought the mirror and set it up. "Everybody stand

back," he shouted. "It's for you alone, Boohoo.

Look and see yourself as you really are."

Boohoo looked into the mirror. "Eh, what's that?" he stammered.

"What's what?" asked Toto.

"That big fat face in the mirror."

"That's you," monkey giggled.

"Oh, no-o, I don't like that. I couldn't look like

that. No one would want to look like that. I don't

like mirrors . . ."

There was anger in hippo's voice. "This is one of
your nasty jokes. I don't like it at all.
'Quite a handsome hippopotamus,' he said.
What a silly idea to think I'd look like that.
You thought you'd fool me, didn't you . . .?"

"Put the mirror on the ground."

"But why?" asked Toto.

"Just put it down there," ordered hippo.

"But what are you going to do?"

"Tread on it," shouted Boohoo.

Glass flew in all directions.

"You've smashed it," yelled Toto.

"Ye-es, I don't like mirrors," mumbled hippo.

"You saw your face. Now what about cracking my coconut?" asked Toto.

Boohoo sniffed. "If you must crack jokes don't expect me to crack coconuts."

Boohoo forgot very quickly what he saw in the mirror.

The mirror had told him the truth. What was wrong were the thoughts inside Boohoo's head.

The Bible is God's wonderful mirror. It shows up our wrong doing and the only way to be forgiven. Jesus made it possible. The great mirror tells how he lived and died and came back to life.

Make a habit of looking into it. This is the way to true happiness.

Read James' letter chapter 1, verses 23 to 26.

91

The Cool Pool

"It's beautiful," said Dic-dic the antelope.

"Um, there's no place like it anywhere," mumbled Boohoo the hippo.

"You're both right," nodded giraffe. "Elephant made it specially for us because we are his friends."

"Er, um, I don't think we deserve it," said hippo.

"Plop!"

A pebble landed in the middle of the Cool Pool and Koko the small monkey strolled into view.

94

She picked up a paw-full of pebbles and started tossing them into the Cool Pool. She liked the plopping noises and the splashing sounds. She gurgled happily as little clouds of mud rose slowly from the bottom. Her gleeful chattering suddenly changed to a yell as a very large mouth closed firmly around her tail and dragged her away from the water.

A muffled voice said, "Eh! Stop it, monkey. That's elephant's Cool Pool."

Boohoo backed away three hippo-lengths and then opened his great lips.

Koko tweaked out her tail.

"You big brutal bumble-footed beast!

I'll do what I like, when I like and how I like."

She put out her tongue at him and scampered up a palm tree.

When the others had walked away and she thought no one was looking she started to throw lumps of mud into the Cool Pool. Then giggling to herself she pulled up the flowers and ferns that grew near the edge and threw them in, roots and all.

As she stood back to admire her work, she saw elephant standing and watching. With a gasp, she shot up a tree and leaped from limb to limb till there was no jump left in her legs.

Days went by and it was Koko's birthday.

Giraffe's head appeared beside her.

"Happy birthday, Koko."

Small monkey jumped onto Twiga's neck and chuckled.

"Today's my latest birthday.

I have two every year now. It helps me to grow up quicker."

"Now that's true monkey-wisdom," smiled Twiga. "Oh, Koko,

I came to tell you that elephant wants to see you."

Koko gulped, jumped down and bolted.

Under the umbrella-tree she met Dic-dic.

Wedged between his horns was a yellow jungle-fruit.

"Koko, happy birthday, here's a present for you."

Small monkey grabbed it. She said nothing for a while; her mouth was too full.

Then she mumbled, "Birthdays are great.

I'll have three every year in future . . ."

Dic-dic laughed, "Did you hear that elephant is looking for you?"

"What does he want me for?" asked Koko trying to look innocent.

"He wants to give you a present," said Dic-dic. "But you don't deserve it. Think of what you did to elephant's Cool Pool."

"I didn't," stammered monkey, but then she remembered that elephant had seen her.

She walked down the path feeling sadly that this wasn't as good a birthday as she had thought.

Hippo smiled at Koko as he came up the path.

"Um, I have a water melon for your birthday."

"Oh, thank you, Boohoo, I love melons. I'm going to have four birthdays a year from now on."

But hippo wasn't listening. He licked his lips. "Um, it isn't easy for a hippo to carry things, so I—um—put it in my mouth and forgot and chewed it.

Lovely flavour—um—delicious."

"You ate my melon?" Koko shouted.

Hippo nodded. "Very delicious it was. But I always say it's the thought that matters. Oh, Koko, did you hear that elephant wants to see you?"

Monkey made a face at him and hurried on.

"She didn't deserve that melon," mumbled hippo shaking his head. "I shouldn't have given it to her."

Round the corner trotted Koko and nearly bumped into elephant.

She stopped, tried to run away, but her legs didn't seem to be able to carry her.

Her mouth felt dry.

"Er—um," she spluttered, and in her mind she saw a picture of the Cool Pool all mud and mess and elephant looking at her.

"Happy birthday," came elephant's big, friendly voice.

Koko looked at the ground and whispered,
"Thank you."

"Look," said elephant. "I have a present for you."

Koko glanced up and saw a bunch of beautiful, ripe bananas.

She stretched out her paws and then shook her head. In a very small voice she said, "I made a mess of the Cool Pool, Tembo, I'm sorry."

There was a big pause.

"I don't deserve to be given a present."

"But this is my gift to you because I love you. When you were sorry, I forgave you, but even before that the bananas had been picked for you."

Koko was feeling very small inside.

"Thank you, Tembo."

She looked at the bunch of bananas. It was as big as she was. "Thank you very much," she smiled. "I'm going back to the pond to clear up as well as I can."

Elephant's eyes were smiling. Koko didn't see. She was still feeling very small.

"I don't deserve it," she whispered.

As she carried her bananas down the jungle path she thought, "I'll share Tembo's gift with hippo and Twiga and Dic-dic." She did, and it was the best birthday she'd ever had.

God's wonderful kindness to us—called grace—is forgiving our sins and giving us everlasting life.

We don't deserve it, we can't earn it or buy it.

It is a free gift to *us* but it cost Jesus His life.

He died on the cross but He came back to life to prove He is God's son.

The wise person accepts His wonderful gift. Take it now.

The Bible tells us a lot about grace.
Read about it in Ephesians, chapter 2, verses 4 to 9.

The Monkeys and the Eggs

Toto and Koko the monkey twins were nearly always hungry. They would eat nuts and berries, fruit and beetles, hairy caterpillars and scorpions, but particularly eggs.

In a very old-looking buyu tree
they saw an old-looking nest.
"Aah," smiled Toto, "where you find nests you find . . .!"
"Eggs," giggled Koko, as Toto climbed the tree, looked into the nest
and came back carrying a rather grubby egg.

He threw it to Koko who clutched at it but missed.

The somewhat soiled egg fell and broke with a loud popping noise on a limb below them. The gooey, greenish stuff which dripped heavily to the ground brought joy to the flies but to no one else in the jungle.

The little monkeys scampered off holding their noses.

Twiga, Boohoo and Dic-dic watched what was going on.

"Eh—how does a good egg become a bad one?" mumbled Boohoo.

Giraffe chuckled, "Just leave it and it will go bad all by itself."

"Um—well, how does a bad egg become good?"

"It doesn't happen," said Dic-dic.

Twiga nodded. "It certainly doesn't happen to eggs."

The monkey twins' Uncle Nyani was walking down the path to the river. In his paw, held very daintily, was an egg, still warm from the nest of Kuku the hen.

He licked his lips.

With great care he made a small hole in the egg, put it in his mouth and sucked with purpose and strength. His cheeks hollowed and his eyes stood out as he sucked.

The small monkeys watched him with envy. When the shell was completely empty Nyani threw it untidily to the ground—a well-known habit of some monkeys.

He sighed contentedly and said, "Eggs are a comfort and joy to a monkey's stomach"—his tongue went all the way round his lips—"that is, *some* eggs are!"

He wound his tail firmly round the limb and shook his finger at the small monkeys.

They listened open-mouthed.

His voice gradually grew louder.

"Some eggs offend the nose.

"They are sadness to the mouth.

"They can be an insult to the inner monkey."

Toto and Koko nodded and asked, "But how can you tell which eggs are which, O wise monkey?"

Nyani chose his words carefully. He held an imaginary egg between thumb and finger. "Some look at an egg; they hold it between their eye and the sun. But be warned, the sharpest eye may be mistaken."

"Some listen." Nyani held the imaginary egg to his ear. "A way of small accuracy."

He leant forwards. "Believe it or not, there are those of smaller monkey-wisdom who crack the shell and sniff."

The monkey twins shook their heads sadly and Koko said in her most sugary voice, "How does a monkey of experience like you deal with this problem?"

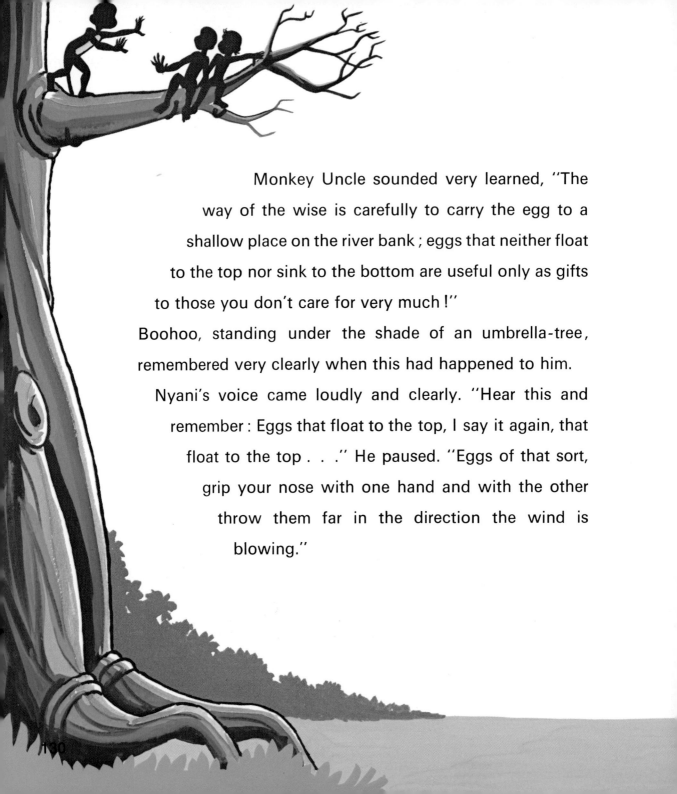

Monkey Uncle sounded very learned, "The way of the wise is carefully to carry the egg to a shallow place on the river bank; eggs that neither float to the top nor sink to the bottom are useful only as gifts to those you don't care for very much!"

Boohoo, standing under the shade of an umbrella-tree, remembered very clearly when this had happened to him.

Nyani's voice came loudly and clearly. "Hear this and remember: Eggs that float to the top, I say it again, that float to the top . . ." He paused. "Eggs of that sort, grip your nose with one hand and with the other throw them far in the direction the wind is blowing."

131

Twiga and Boohoo and Dic-dic watched the old monkey swinging along through the branches.

Giraffe nodded, "There was wisdom in his words."

"Oh, yes!" agreed hippo. "But I'm very disappointed that you can't make a bad egg into a . . . er . . . good one."

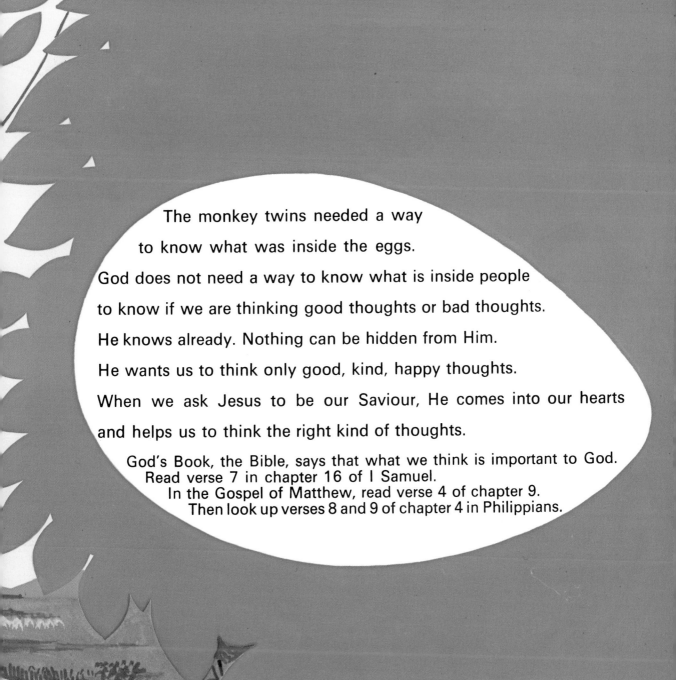

The monkey twins needed a way

to know what was inside the eggs.

God does not need a way to know what is inside people

to know if we are thinking good thoughts or bad thoughts.

He knows already. Nothing can be hidden from Him.

He wants us to think only good, kind, happy thoughts.

When we ask Jesus to be our Saviour, He comes into our hearts

and helps us to think the right kind of thoughts.

God's Book, the Bible, says that what we think is important to God.
Read verse 7 in chapter 16 of I Samuel.
In the Gospel of Matthew, read verse 4 of chapter 9.
Then look up verses 8 and 9 of chapter 4 in Philippians.

Monkey Crosses the Equator

Toto the monkey was visiting his relations who lived in a place in the deep jungle where the trees were tall and the leaves were very green and butterflies hovered over the water-lilies.

39

Toto came to an extremely large buyu tree. Underneath it was a notice board beside the road which read EQUATOR.

Twiga the giraffe came close to him. "This is a very interesting place, little monkey."

"Er, yes," mumbled Boohoo the hippo. "It's the middle of the world."

EQUATOR

141

Monkey's eyes were full of excitement. "The very middle?"

"Yes," nodded Twiga. "Sit where you are in the buyu tree and you're in the Southern Hemisphere, but if you walk down that long limb and jump into the kuyu tree then you'll be in the Northern Hemisphere. You will have crossed the equator."

Toto scratched his head. This was a difficult thing for monkeys to understand.

He had heard much about the North and the wonderful things that were there.

Thoughts swirled round in his brain. He wanted to go that way, and here he was very close.

All he had to do was to jump and he'd be there.

He wondered what it would feel like to be in the North.

Exciting little tingles started between his ears and scampered right down to his tail.

He walked up and down the limb talking softly to himself and thinking of how different he would soon feel.

145

From the shadows came a voice, a soft, sugary, hissy sort of voice. "It will be wonderful, little monkey. Keep thinking how different it's all going to feel. You will know you're there because you'll be full of a wonderful joy."

146

Giraffe and hippo, who were standing in the shade, listened and watched anxiously.

There was a dreamy look in little monkey's eyes.

"That's snake," said Twiga. "He knows you've decided to cross the equator so now he wants to try and spoil it for you.

"Don't take any notice of the cunning of snakes. The North's the place," Twiga went on, "it's Elephant's country.

"When you're close to him you're safe. It's the place of real happiness.

"If you trust him, he always does what he promises."

Toto thought of Twiga and elephant and a warm feeling spread through his monkey body.

He ran along the limb shouting, "I'm going north."

He jumped far out and landed safely on a limb of the kuyu tree.

He felt no bump as he crossed the equator.

He crouched in the kuyu tree quivering with excitement.

He'd done it.

He was in the North!

Old things were behind.

Everything would be different now. He waited for it to happen.

But he felt the same, exactly the same. The same wind blew on him, the same sun shone down. Had he really crossed over that line?

From down below under the kuyu tree came snake's voice, very coaxingly, "It's all a leg-pull, little friend. Come down here, I know the path you want. Thrills, excitement, adventure, tingling feelings, doing things and not being found out. You'll feel wonderful."

The enticing voice seemed to draw him down. Then he saw hippo and Twiga and Dic-dic the antelope looking up at him anxiously.

"Er, Toto," came hippo's voice, "don't forget the day when you looked into snake's eyes."

Toto suddenly thought of the terrible day when he had done that and had nearly become snake's dinner. He heard giraffe's voice, kindly and close to him.

"Toto, you may not *feel* different, but use your eyes. You are now in the kuyu tree and the kuyu tree is in the Northern Hemisphere. Geography is geography."

Toto nodded doubtfully, but his monkey mind still felt dizzy. "Twiga, surely I should feel different if this North is what you say it is?"

Toto sat on a wide piece of the limb. He read the notice forwards and backwards. He read it hanging by his arms and hanging by his tail. It said the same thing every time. He felt the kuyu tree firm beneath his paws. "Surely," he said out loud, "surely, it *is* so. I am in the Northern Hemisphere, and I don't *feel* any different."

Twiga's head was very close to him. "Facts are facts, little monkey. Kuyu trees are kuyu trees."

"Um, yes," agreed Boohoo, "um—why don't you continue in a northerly direction?"

"He's right, you know," nodded Twiga, "the further you go, the more you will know where you are and where you're going, and the more you'll feel it."

"Er, yes," said Boohoo, "didn't elephant say, the further you go the better you'll know?"

Toto took their advice, and the way things turned out he was so glad that he had.

When we believe in Jesus as our Saviour, our faces look the same, our voices sound the same, and our bodies feel the same. But we are different deep inside:

We have become a new child of God.

Our sins are all washed away.

We have new life that will never end.

We know this is true because *God says* it is so,

not because *we feel* it is so.

Read for yourself what God has said:
In the Gospel of John, chapter 1, verse 12.
In the first Letter of John, chapter 2, verse 12.
In the Gospel of John, chapter 3, verse 16.
In the Gospel of John, chapter 5, verse 24.

Sweet and Sour Hippo

It was a lovely day beside the lake in the jungle. Toto the monkey and Twiga the giraffe were full of joy. They watched zebras and antelopes grazing in the shade and drinking the cool water of the lake.

"Oh, ooh," chattered Toto, "look who's coming."

Twiga smiled. "The best way to be unhappy and to stay that way is to think the thoughts that Boohoo the hippo is thinking at this moment."

"Poor old Boohoo," chuckled Toto, "he's a mountain of misery. Let's see if we can cheer him up and make him smile."

161

Hippo's grumbly voice came. "Where's my fruit? It was here on the top of the rock, now it's gone. What did you do with it, monkey?"

"Boohoo, I didn't take your food," said Toto.

"He's telling the truth," said Twiga. "Goon the baboon stole it. I saw him."

"Oh, um . . ." muttered Boohoo, "you can't trust anybody in the jungle these days. It's terrible, I was looking forward to some nice fruit."

"Isn't it a lovely sunny day, Boohoo?" said Twiga.

"Um, er . . . I dislike the hot sun, it makes my skin sore, and it itches and twitches, you wouldn't believe . . ." He shook his head sadly. "And then there's my nose, I sneeze and I wheeze and my nose runs. Um, eh . . . look out! I'm going to . . . to snee . . . to sneeze!"

Toto jumped down and pressed on Hippo's upper lip.

Boohoo blinked. "Oh, eh, thank you, Toto. If I start sneezing my nose runs, my eyes run, my—eh . . ."

"Aren't the jungle flowers beautiful these days, Boohoo?" said Twiga.

"I think they smell beautiful," said Toto.

"Um . . ." mumbled Boohoo, "I don't like those little yellow flowers, or the pink ones, they make me sneeze, you see. Then my nose blocks up and it itches and twitches and I wheeze and sneeze and—um . . ."

"Yes, yes," sighed Twiga, "now just come and sit in the shade and enjoy this cool breeze."

"Yes," agreed Toto, "what a difference that breeze makes to the jungle."

"Yes," mumbled Hippo, "an awful difference. It brings the stuff out of those little flowers, it goes up my nose and my nose starts to itch and twitch and . . ." He shook his head sorrowfully. "If you only knew how much I ache when I sneeze, my ribs ache when I wheeze and my nose gets blocked and my eyes run and . . . did I tell you about my ears?"

169

"If you must suffer," said Toto, "please suffer in silence."

"Oh, I don't mind suffering in silence as long as everybody knows I'm suffering in silence."

Toto put his fingers in his ears. "Oh, you big bumpy, lumpy, grumpy beast."

"Who are you calling names?"

"You," sniffed Toto. "You haven't the brains of a donkey!"

"Have you?"

"Of course I have!"

"Haw, haw, haw," Boohoo laughed, and then stopped suddenly. "Aw, that makes my ribs sore too, and oh my back, it—um . . ."

"Why don't you go and have another swim in the lake?" suggested Twiga.

"There are too many animals down there already, and they're unfriendly, they don't talk to you. I try to be friendly, put in a cheerful word here and there but they take no notice, they walk away."

Twiga tried again.

"Look down at the lake, what do you see?"

"I see Dic-dic the antelope, swimming and splashing," said Toto.

Twiga stretched his neck and looked carefully into the distance.

"I've been watching a long brown log floating on top of the lake."

Boohoo shook his head slowly. "There aren't any logs in that lake."

"But I can see it," said Toto.

"Um, listen," said Boohoo, "I've been all over the lake and there aren't any logs anywhere."

"Oh, go on," snapped Toto, "open your big mouth, start another argument. You're about as welcome as a crocodile in a swimming hole."

"Ooh, am I, a crocodile in a swimming hole eh? Crocodile!"

"Can you see that log, Twiga?"

"Yes, it's floating towards little antelope."

Boohoo lifted his head high, there was a gleam in his eye and his voice was strong and eager. "It isn't a log, it's Crunch the crocodile, and he's after antelope. I'll stop him, I can swim and I can bite. Here's where hippos come in handy." He dashed down the hill, dived into the water, and swam powerfully.

Toto shivered. "How can he fight crocodile?"

"Boohoo swims like a fish," said Twiga.

"But crocodiles bite!"

"And so do hippos, with mouths twice as big as crocodiles. Look, crocodile has seen him, and now he's going in the other direction."

175

176

Toto danced with joy. "He saved the antelope, good old Boohoo, three cheers for hippo!" He stopped and scratched his head. "Can this strong, brave, fast-moving animal be that moaning, groaning, mumbling, grumbling hippo that everybody tried to avoid? Twiga, how can he be sour at one moment and sweet the next?"

Giraffe smiled. "I'm proud of him. When Boohoo thinks of himself and his troubles, he becomes a sighing, miserable skinful of self-pity. But he stopped being sour when he forgot himself and started to think of someone else."

"Thank you, Boohoo," cried Dic-dic, "oh, thank you! You helped so much and rescued me and protected me too."

"Oh—um—did I?" Hippo smiled. "Isn't it a lovely day? Er . . . isn't it good to be alive?"

How big our problems grow when we keep on thinking about them! But there is no need to keep on worrying. God wants us to tell Him about our problems and to trust Him to take care of us.

Then we will be able to stop thinking about ourselves and to start thinking about others and how we can help them.

Many people have problems much bigger than ours.

How happy they will be to know we love them,

and that God loves them, too!

God has told us of His love many times in the Bible.
Find verse 7 in chapter 5 of I Peter.
Look in I John for verse 11 of chapter 4.
In Philippians, chapter 2, verse 4, we are told to think of others, not just of ourselves.

Jungle Doctor CARTOONS

The adventures of Toto the Monkey, Hippo, Twiga and the other jungle animals continue in Jungle Doctor Cartoons Collection. Twelve more stories

presented in full-colour strip cartoons invite you to share the lessons they learn. Why don't you join the animals and find out more...

ISBN 1 85078 268 7 paperback 64 pages

OM publishing

THE GREAT BIBLE DISCOVERY

Alive & kicking

If you think **Genesis** is the name of a rock group, **Exodus** was a Bob Marley song and **Revelation** is something that happens when your Dad's wig blows off . . . it's time for a re-think . . it's time you took **The Great Bible Discovery** home with you. Where can you meet **two kings**, up to **21 Judges** and witness a mass **Exodus** before getting in on the Acts? **The Great Bible Discovery** - it could be a Revelation in your living room.

4 VOLUMES TO COLLECT

OM PUBLISHING